The Banza

A Haitian story by
DIANE WOLKSTEIN

Pictures by
MARC BROWN

Dial Books for Young Readers
New York

Published by Dial Books for Young Readers
A Division of Penguin Books USA Inc.
375 Hudson Street
New York, New York 10014
Text copyright © 1981 by Diane Wolkstein
Pictures copyright © 1981 by Marc Brown
All rights reserved. Typography by Atha Tehon
Printed in Hong Kong by South China Printing Company
COBE
5 7 9 10 8 6 4

Library of Congress Cataloging in Publication Data
Wolkstein, Diane.
The banza: a Haitian story.
Summary: A small goat finds that the banjo given to her by
a little tiger protects her from harm in an unexpected way.
(1. Folklore—Haiti.) I. Brown, Marc Tolon, ill. II. Title.
PZ8.1.W84Ban   398.2'45297358'097294   (E)   81-65845
ISBN 0-8037-0428-3   AACR2
ISBN 0-8037-0429-1 (lib. bdg.)

The art for each picture consists of a key drawing with
three overlays prepared in pencil, felt-tip marker, and gouache
and reproduced in black, blue, yellow, and red halftone.

For Mme. Gurewich,
who teaches the big and small song
and always the song of the heart
D. W.

To Nancy Bryan,
who saved me from becoming
a brain surgeon
M. B.

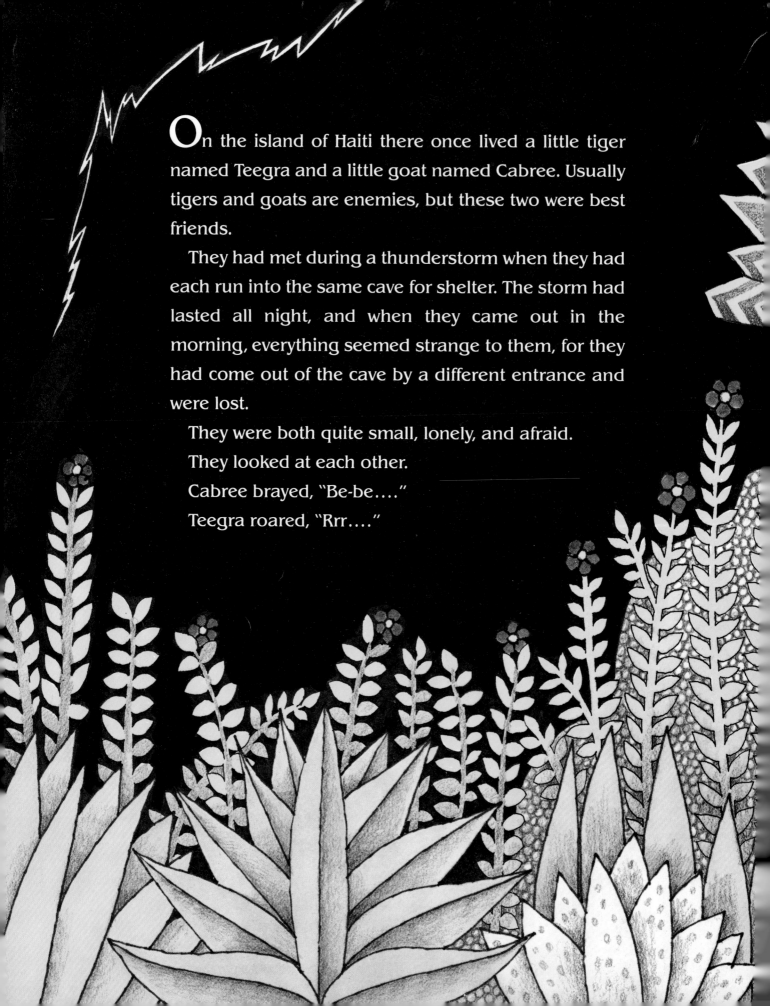

On the island of Haiti there once lived a little tiger named Teegra and a little goat named Cabree. Usually tigers and goats are enemies, but these two were best friends.

They had met during a thunderstorm when they had each run into the same cave for shelter. The storm had lasted all night, and when they came out in the morning, everything seemed strange to them, for they had come out of the cave by a different entrance and were lost.

They were both quite small, lonely, and afraid.

They looked at each other.

Cabree brayed, "Be-be...."

Teegra roared, "Rrr...."

"Do you want to be friends?" Cabree asked.

"Now!" Teegra answered.

So they wandered over the countryside, playing together, sharing whatever food they found, and sleeping close to each other at night for warmth.

Then one morning they found themselves in front of the cave where they had first met.

"rrRRRRR!"

Cabree turned. But it was not Teegra who had roared.

"RRRRRRrrr-rrRR!"

It was a roar of another tiger.

"Mama! Papa! *Auntie!*" Teegra cried joyfully as three huge tigers bounded out of the bushes.

Cabree ran into the cave without waiting.

After a while Teegra went to find Cabree, but Cabree refused to come out of the cave, so Teegra went home with his family.

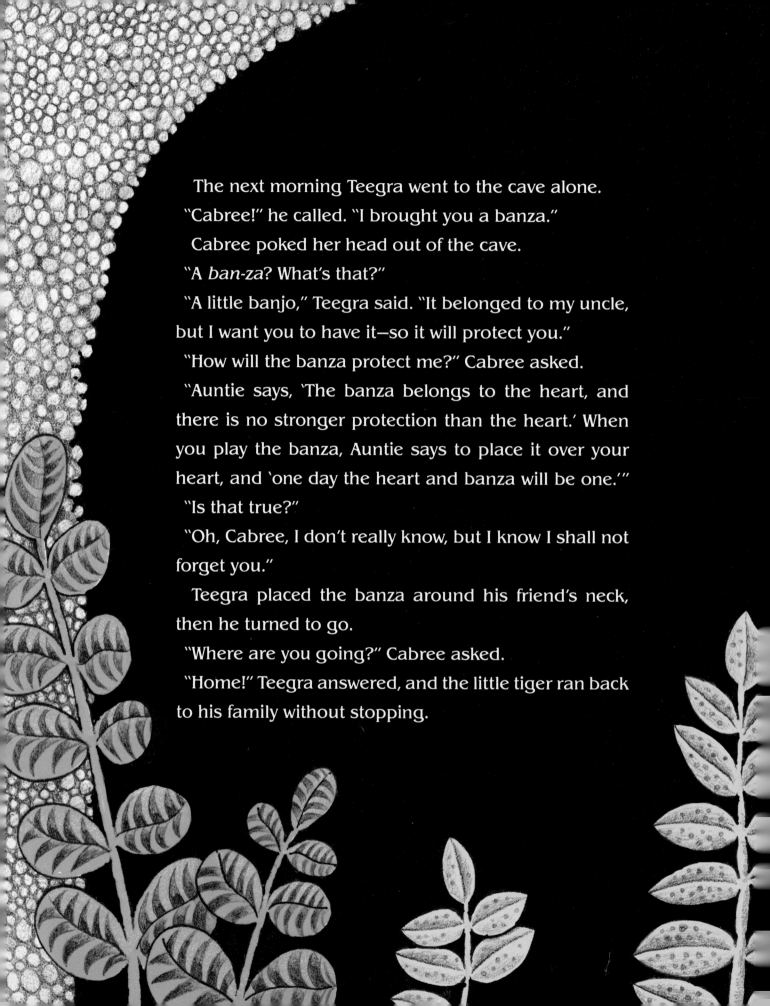

The next morning Teegra went to the cave alone.

"Cabree!" he called. "I brought you a banza."

Cabree poked her head out of the cave.

"A *ban-za*? What's that?"

"A little banjo," Teegra said. "It belonged to my uncle, but I want you to have it—so it will protect you."

"How will the banza protect me?" Cabree asked.

"Auntie says, 'The banza belongs to the heart, and there is no stronger protection than the heart.' When you play the banza, Auntie says to place it over your heart, and 'one day the heart and banza will be one.'"

"Is that true?"

"Oh, Cabree, I don't really know, but I know I shall not forget you."

Teegra placed the banza around his friend's neck, then he turned to go.

"Where are you going?" Cabree asked.

"Home!" Teegra answered, and the little tiger ran back to his family without stopping.

Cabree stepped out of the cave so she could see the banza more clearly. It was a beautiful banza, and when the sun shone on it, it gleamed. Cabree held the banza over her heart. She stroked it gently. A friendly, happy sound came out. She stroked it again—and again—and before she realized it, she was trotting through the forest, humming to herself and stopping now and then to play a tune on the banza.

One afternoon Cabree came to a spring. She wanted to drink, but she was afraid the banza would get wet, so she took it off and carefully laid it down in the bushes. As she drank the cool sweet water she heard a low growl behind her.

"rrrRRrrr...."

Turning quickly, Cabree saw four large hungry tigers.
Cabree wanted to leap across the stream and run away,
but the banza was in the bushes behind the tigers. No!
She would not leave the banza Teegra had given her.

Slowly and fiercely Cabree walked toward the banza.

Another tiger appeared. Now there were five.

Cabree kept walking.

"Where are you going?" the leader shouted.

Cabree reached the bushes. She picked up the banza and hung it around her neck. Then she turned to the tigers. Five more jumped out of the bushes.

Now there were ten!

"What have you put around your neck?" asked the leader.

And Cabree, trying to quiet her thundering, pounding heart, brought her foreleg to her chest and, by mistake, plucked the banza.

"A musician!" said the chief, laughing. "So you wish to play us a song?"

"No!" said Cabree.

"No?" echoed the leader. And all the tigers took a step closer to Cabree.

Teegra! Cabree wanted to shout. But Teegra was far away, and she was alone, surrounded by the tigers. No, she was not completely alone. She still had the banza Teegra had given her.

Cabree's heart beat very fast, but in time to her heartbeat she stroked the banza. She opened her mouth, and a song came out. To her own surprise it was a loud, low, ferocious song:

> *Ten fat tigers, ten fat tigers,*
> *Cabree eats tigers raw.*
> *Yesterday Cabree ate ten tigers;*
> *Today Cabree eats ten more.*

The tigers were astonished.

"Who is Cabree? And where did you learn that song?" demanded the chief.

"I am Cabree." Cabree answered in a new deep voice, and noticing how frightened the tigers looked, she added, "And that is *my* song. I always sing it before dinner."

The tiger chief realized that three of his tigers had suddenly disappeared.

"Madame Cabree," he said, "you play beautifully. Permit me to offer you a drink."

"Very well," said Cabree.

"Bring Madame Cabree a drink!" he ordered the two tigers closest to him, and as they started to leave he whispered, "and don't come back."

Five tigers stared at Madame Cabree.

Cabree stared back. Then she stroked her banza and sang, a little slower, but just as intently:

Five fat tigers, five fat tigers,
Cabree eats tigers raw.
Yesterday Cabree ate ten tigers;
Today Cabree eats five more.

"Oh! Oh-h-h! Something dreadful must have happened to my tigers," said the leader. "You." He motioned to the two tigers nearest him. "Go fetch Madame Cabree a drink." And again he whispered, "And don't come back."

Now only three tigers quaked before Madame
Cabree. Cabree sang again:

> *Three fat tigers, three fat tigers,*
> *Cabree eats tigers raw.*
> *Yesterday Cabree ate ten tigers;*
> *Today Cabree eats three more.*

When she finished her song, only the leader remained. Cabree began:

One fat tiger—

"Please," whispered the leader, "please let me go. I promise no tiger will ever bother you again."

Cabree looked at the trembling tiger. All she had done was to play the banza and sing what was in her heart. So Teegra's Auntie was right. Her heart had protected her. Her heart and her banza.

"Please!" begged the leader. "I'll do whatever you wish."

"Then go at once to Teegra, the little tiger who lives near the cave. Tell Teegra: 'Today Cabree's heart and the banza are one.'"

"Yes, yes," said the tiger. "'Today Cabree's heart and the banza are one.'" And the tiger chief ran off to find Teegra.

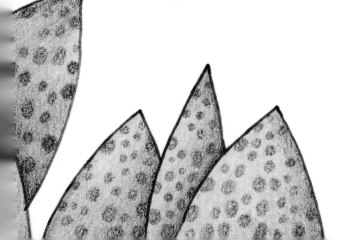
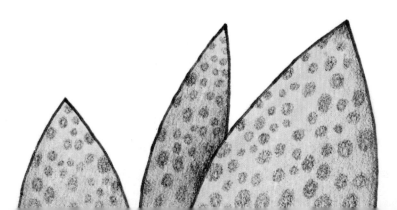

With her banza gleaming around her neck, Cabree went trotting through the forest. But every now and then she would stop. She would stroke her banza and sing, for her heart would have a new song.

Author's Note

Sitting on a stone wall outside the home of Mme. Bellande in Diquini, Haiti, Antoine Exavier told stories one evening in 1973 to Mme. Bellande; my daughter, Rachel; and myself. He began each story by shouting out the word *"CRIC?"* and we, eager to hear each story, shouted back each time *"CRAC!"* Antoine called this story "Teegra—Cabree" (pronounced *TEE-gra* and *CAH-bree*), which means "tiger" and "goat" in Creole.

The story stayed with me because of the little goat's silly song, the love shared between the tiger and the goat, and the strange yet beautiful sounding name of an instrument called the *banza*. When I questioned Haitians about the banza, no one seemed to know any more about it than that it was an "old instrument." (Indeed, Dena J. Epstein, in the series *Music in American Life,* cites documents proving that the banjo originated in Africa and was played in Haiti in the eighteenth century as a hollowed-out calabash with hemp strings called a banza.) That Teegra receives the banza from his uncle also implies it belongs to the heritage, for religious tradition (Voodoo) in Haiti is usually passed by the uncles rather than the fathers. When Cabree makes the banza sing, not only is she expressing her own feelings and humor, but she is also continuing the tradition as well as joining herself to the one from whom she is separated. The ageless themes of love, community, and self-expression are interwoven into this friendly, lively, and often very funny Haitian folktale.

I hope that whoever tells *The Banza* will call out *"CRIC?"* and those who are listening will call back *"CRAC!"*

D.W.

Artist's Note

In the illustrations for *The Banza* I have incorporated the elements basic to Haitian art—bright colors, flat shapes, varied patterns—as well as many of the symbols that pervade that art: the palm trees that symbolize joy and liberty, the flowers that signify precious freedoms, even certain Voodoo symbols. The exotic animals that appear in *The Banza* are also found throughout the art of this Caribbean island, reflecting its African and European heritage.

Most of all I have tried to convey the spirit of Haitian art, which is alive with personal, spontaneous feeling, innocent rather than primitive, and always reflective of the artist's own experience.

M.B.